Who are you, Baby Kangaroo?

written by Stella Blackstone
illustrated by Clare Beaton

Barefoot Books
Celebrating Art and Story

"Who are you, baby kangaroo?"
"I'm not going to tell you. You'll have to ask...

...the wolf cubs."

"Wolf cubs, wolf cubs, can you give me a clue?

Can you tell me the name of the baby kangaroo?"

"Oh no, we don't know. Why don't you ask...

...the cygnets?"

"Cygnets, cygnets, can you give me a clue?

Can you tell me the name of the baby kangaroo?"

"Oh no, we don't know. Why don't you ask...

...the piglets?"

"Piglets, piglets, can you give me a clue?

Can you tell me the name of the baby kangaroo?"

"Oh no, we don't know. Why don't you ask...

...the penguin chicks?"
"Penguin chicks, penguin chicks, can you give me a clue?
Can you tell me the name of the baby kangaroo?"
"Oh no, we don't know. Why don't you ask...

...the moose calves?"

"Moose calves, moose calves, can you give me a clue?
Can you tell me the name of the baby kangaroo?"

"Oh no, we don't know. Why don't you ask...

...the zebra foals?"

"Zebra foals, zebra foals, can you give me a clue?

Can you tell me the name of the baby kangaroo?"

"Oh no, we don't know. Why don't you ask...

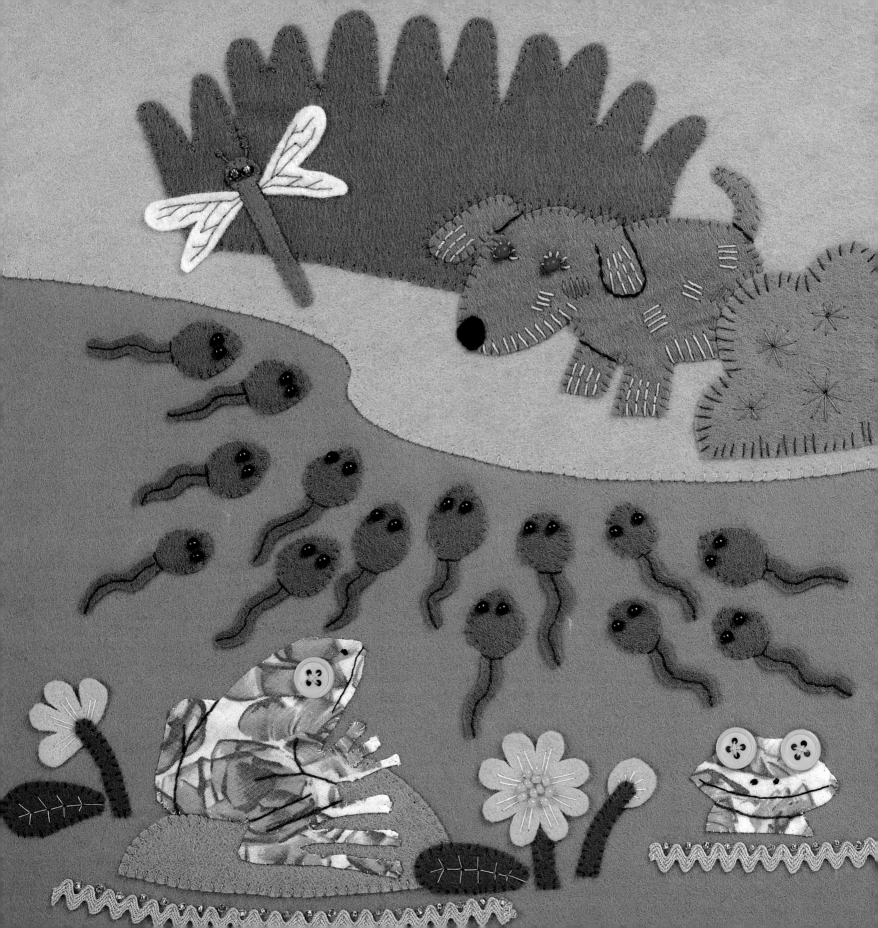

...the tadpoles?"

"Tadpoles, tadpoles, can you give me a clue?
Can you tell me the name of the baby kangaroo?"
"Oh no, we don't know. Why don't you ask...

...the woolly lambs?"
"Woolly lambs, woolly lambs, can you give me a clue?
Can you tell me the name of the baby kangaroo?"
"Oh no, we don't know. Why don't you ask...

...the beaver kittens?"

"Beaver kittens, beaver kittens, can you give me a clue?

Can you tell me the name of the baby kangaroo?"

"Oh no, we don't know. Why don't you ask...

...his mother?"
"What a good idea!
Tell me, tell me, Mommy Kangaroo,
What is the name of your baby kangaroo?"

"You've traveled all around the world looking for a clue. Your answer is not far away. My baby kangaroo is...

…a joey!
And tell me, little puppy, where's your mom, and who are you?"

"Here she comes to fetch me with my brothers, small and new.
Thank you for helping me, Mommy Kangaroo!"

The Animals and their Babies

Wolves – wolf cubs
(North America, Europe, Asia and the Arctic)
Wolves live together in families or packs that travel and
hunt together. Usually just the leaders have cubs, but
the whole pack helps to raise them. One litter of three
to six cubs is born every year in an underground den.
Wolf cubs cannot see or hear when they are born but
after a few weeks they are busy exploring outside.

Swans – cygnets
(everywhere except Antarctica)
Swans mate for life and build huge nests on the ground
near water. They lay between three and eight eggs at
one time. After they have hatched, the cygnets are very
helpless and keep close to their parents, even getting lifts
on their backs. They learn to fly when they're about four
months old.

Pigs – piglets
(worldwide)
Mother pigs are called sows, and usually give birth twice
a year to a litter of piglets numbering anything from six
to twenty five (the record is over thirty!) Sows lie down
and grunt to let their piglets know when it is feeding time.
The last piglet to be born is the smallest and is called
the "runt."

Penguins – penguin chicks
(Antarctica)

The female penguin lays one egg, which the male looks after for two months. He holds it under his feet to keep it warm. When the egg hatches the male goes off to feed while the female looks after the chick. Later the two parents take turns feeding their chick. The chicks form groups called "crèches" huddling together to keep warm. They go for their first swim when they are about two months old.

Moose – moose calves
(North America)

Moose cows usually give birth to twins, and sometimes triplets. Normally calm, quiet animals that avoid people, they can become very angry when protecting their young. The mother makes a long cough-like moaning sound to gather her calves to her.

Zebra – zebra foals
(Africa)

A new zebra foal can stand up on his long wobbly legs within fifteen minutes of being born. The mother has just one baby at a time. The foals are born with a light brown background color to their stripes instead of the white we see on adults. This helps them to hide from hungry lions and hyenas.

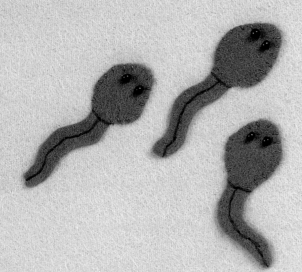

Frogs – tadpoles
(worldwide)

In the spring, frogs lay hundreds of eggs, called frogspawn, in ponds. Within a few weeks, the frogspawn turns into tadpoles. The tadpoles then grow legs, lose their tails and become tiny frogs. Many tadpoles get eaten by fish, birds and other animals and this is why so many eggs need to be laid.

Sheep – lambs
(worldwide)

Ewes (female sheep) normally give birth once a year, and have one to three lambs. The mother knows her lamb by its smell and the lamb recognizes its mother by her bleat. Lambs are very playful and run and skip about together.

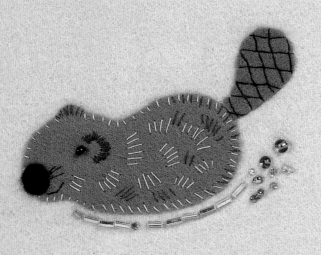

Beavers – beaver kittens
(North America)

Beavers usually have litters of four or five kittens. Beaver kittens are born with lots of fur and with their eyes open. They can get into the water as soon as half an hour after birth, and are good swimmers within a week. On land, the mother often carries the kittens around on her broad tail as she walks.

Kangaroos – joeys

(Australia)

When joeys are born, they are very tiny — only 2.5cm long. Just one baby is born at a time, and it lives in its mother's pouch, suckling and growing for about ten months. After leaving the pouch, it still feeds from its mother for another six months — running about and jumping in and out of the pouch whenever it's hungry or frightened.

Dogs – puppies

(worldwide)

Litters of puppies vary in size — the largest ever recorded was of twenty three puppies! Like kittens, puppies are born with their eyes closed and do not open them for at least a week. They are not color blind, but see the world in the same way that we see it at twilight.

for Natasha, Brendan and Noah — S. B.
for Joanna and her enthusiasm — C. B.

Barefoot Books
2067 Massachusetts Ave
Cambridge, MA 02140

Text copyright © 2004 by Stella Blackstone
Illustrations copyright © 2004 by Clare Beaton
The moral right of Stella Blackstone to be identified as the author
and Clare Beaton to be identified as the illustrator of this work has been asserted

First published in the United States of America in 2004 by Barefoot Books, Inc.
This book was typeset in Plantin Schoolbook Bold 21 on 31 point
The illustrations were prepared in antique fabrics and felt
with sequins, buttons, beads and assorted bric-a-brac

Graphic design by Judy Linard, London
Color separation by Bright Arts, Singapore
Printed and bound in Singapore by Tien Wah Press (Pte) Ltd

This book has been printed on 100% acid-free paper

Library of Congress Cataloging-in-Publication Data

Blackstone, Stella.
Who are you, baby kangaroo? / written by Stella Blackstone ; illustrated by Clare Beaton.
    p. cm.
    Summary: A curious puppy leads the reader to a number of animal babies in search of the name for a baby
kangaroo. Includes notes on animal mothers and various infant animals.
ISBN 1-84148-217-X
    [1. Animals--Names--Fiction. 2. Animals--Infancy--Fiction. 3. Stories in rhyme.] I. Beaton, Clare, ill. II. Title.

PZ8.3.B5735Wm 2004
  [E]--dc22

                        2004004652

                        1 3 5 7 9 8 6 4 2

Barefoot Books
Celebrating Art and Story

At Barefoot Books, we celebrate art and story with books that open the hearts and minds of children from all walks of life, inspiring them to read deeper, search further, and explore their own creative gifts. Taking our inspiration from many different cultures, we focus on themes that encourage independence of spirit, enthusiasm for learning, and acceptance of other traditions. Thoughtfully prepared by writers, artists and storytellers from all over the world, our products combine the best of the present with the best of the past to educate our children as the caretakers of tomorrow.

www.barefootbooks.com